Hooray! Hooray!
I sit! I stay!

HODDER CHILDREN'S BOOKS

First published in Great Britain in 2016 by Hodder and Stoughton

Text copyright © Mick Inkpen 2016
Illustrations copyright © Chloë Inkpen 2016

Hodder Children's Books
An imprint of Hachette Children's Group
Part of Hodder and Stoughton
Carmelite House
50 Victoria Embankment
London EC4Y 0DZ

A CIP catalogue record for this book is available from the British Library.

ISBN 978 1 444 92952 2

Printed in China

An Hachette UK Company
www.hachette.co.uk

Fred

Mick & Chloë Inkpen

Hodder
Children's
Books

I am not best in class.
But I'm not last!
I passed my test
along with all the rest.
At last I stay away
from cars and poo!
I know just what to do.
When called to come
I do not run away!

(Not often anyway.)

And I can fetch a stick.
Or ball.
I come when called.
And that's not all. . .

I sit! I stay!

I do not
run away.

Hooray!

'Fetch!'
   and 'Sit!'
and 'Stay!'.
 I understand them all.
Those are the words I know.

And 'Ball!'
   and 'Walk!'
and 'Park!'
   and 'Bed!'.
I know those too.

But what is. . .

'Fred! Fred! Fred!' they say.
They say it all the time.
'Fred! Fred! Fred!' all day.
(You whisper it sometimes.)

If only I could Fred.
But Fred? It makes no sense.
They laugh and shake their heads.
They say I'm dense.

But I will Fred one day.
I know I will.
If I can Fetch and Sit and Stay,
I'll Fred. I know I will.
And they will clap and say,
'Good Boy!'

I know they will.

There is another dog upstairs
where I am not allowed to go.
I saw him once.
I wonder if he knows
what Fred is all about
and why they shout it
all the time.

He looks like me!
He has my ball.
He has no smell at all.

I'm chasing pigeons in the park
which I am not allowed to do.
I like the way they flap about.
I think they like it too.

And if there ar

...no pigeons, a duck will have to do!

There is that other
dog again!
The dog I saw
the other day!
And look!
He has my ball again!
I wonder if he wants to

play!

Paddle!
Struggle!
Bubble!
Trouble!
Kick!
And splutter!
Choke!
And sink. . .

'Fred!'

I hear.
But cannot
think.

A scream!

A dash!

A jump!

A splash!

A foot!

A face. . .

...it's you!

I'm safe!

I shake the water
from my ears.
I lick your face.
I taste your tears.

'Oh Fred,' you whisper,
'Fred. Fred. Fred.'

A **light** goes on inside my head!

I stare into your eyes
and blink.
I think a thought,
a thought that thinks . . .

Fred is a **name!**

Fred is my name!

And suddenly I see
that I am Fred!
That Fred...

...is **me!**

I have been Fredding
all the time!
Fred is a name.

And it is **mine!**

I whizz around.
I make you laugh.
I look at you.
You say I'm daft.

I sit for you.
I lift my paw,
then jump into
your arms once more.

I nudge your nose.
Your cheek is soft.
I try to wag
my tail
right off!

There's nothing left
for me to do,
 except to run
back home
  with you.

I am very fond of you.
You smell pondy too.

I drag my blanket
from my bed,
  and snuggle up
with you instead.

I think
the thought
  inside my head,
the thought
  that **knows**
that I am . . .

. . . Fred.